ISBN 0 86163 159 5

Text and illustrations copyright © 1986
Award Publications Limited,
Spring House, Spring Place,
London NW5 3BH

Printed in Belgium

The Little Yellow Train

by Hayden McAllister

TOOT

Award Publications — London

The Little Yellow Train

It was night time, but not too dark. A yellow moon shone and the stars twinkled as Tom, the engine driver, slept in his cottage on top of Green Hill.

He had his alarm clock set for six o'clock in the morning for he had to be up early to drive the little yellow railway train.

At the bottom of Green Hill was a great big cave. Inside the cave stood the little yellow railway engine, his name was Toot.

The little engine always slept with one eye open.

At seven o'clock, Tom, the engine driver, walked down the Green Hill path to the cave where the little yellow engine slept. He carried some sandwiches and a flask of tea in his train driver's bag.

'Good morning!' said Tom to the yellow engine.

The little engine opened his other eye. He was so pleased to see Tom that his face broke into a great big smile and his whistle went 'Toot Toot!'

'We're off to Flower Valley today,' said Tom with a smile.

Soon the little yellow engine was puffing out of his cave in Green Hill and heading towards Sunny Wood railway station.

A green signal lamp hanging on Oswald Owl's oak tree meant that the line ahead was clear.

The animals in Sunny Wood took care of the Sunny Wood railway track. They wore Sunny Wood railway hats and badges.

If any rocks or sticks fell on the track, the animals of the Sunny Wood railway would move them.

Straight ahead Tom could see the Sunny Wood railway station. He always liked driving the little yellow train through this colourful wood, so full of trees and flowers and grass and happy bird-song.

This morning his passengers were Herbert von Hare, the famous conductor, Maurice Mole, the saxophonist, Willie Mouse, the flute-player and Prudence Pig, the singer.

All four passengers had tickets to Flower Valley which was a long train ride. They were joining the Flower Valley orchestra there for a special concert. So while the little yellow railway train chug-chugged through the country, they entertained themselves.

Willie Mouse blew a tune on his flute, Maurice Mole played the saxophone, and Herbert von Hare conducted and, of course, they played tunes that Prudence Pig could sing, even though her voice was a tiny bit squeaky!

Tom, the driver, was listening to the chug-chug of the little yellow engine, which was music to his ears, when suddenly he saw two red signal lamps hanging from Sam Squirrel's tree ahead.

One red signal lamp meant STOP.
Two meant DANGER!

Tom put on the brakes at once. He wondered what the trouble was. Then directly ahead he saw that a great big tree had fallen right across the railway track.
Sam Squirrel was standing on top of the tree, hopping from one foot to the other and waving a red flag.

When the train came to a halt, all the passengers were
gazing anxiously out of the carriage windows.

'We'll never be able to move that huge tree!' piped
Willie Mouse.

'We'll have to go back to Sunny Wood station!'
squeaked Prudence Pig.

'My hat! We'll be late for our concert at Flower
Valley!' cried Herbert von Hare.

'Tut Tut!' said the little yellow railway engine.

Signalman Sam Squirrel came skipping down the track to see Tom.

'The tree fell on the track last night with a crash like thunder!' he gasped. 'And . . .' he went on, still waving his flag — 'seven of our strongest Sunny Wood rabbits couldn't even budge it!'

'Don't worry,' said Tom. 'We'll think of something!'

Soon the passengers had gathered around the fallen tree. Herbert von Hare was very cross. 'I'll be late for my concert!' he muttered.

'We shall all be late for our concert, don't you mean?' corrected Maurice Mole.

'What shall we do?' asked Willie Mouse anxiously.

'I say we get a woodpecker to peck a big hole in the tree,' squeaked Prudence Pig.

While they were all talking, Tom found a piece of strong rope in his driver's cab. He tied one end around the trunk of the big tree. The other end he tied to a hook underneath the little yellow engine.

'Stand back everybody,' Tom cried.

Then he climbed into the cab, and put the yellow engine into reverse.

'Puff-puff-puff-puff'. The yellow train started to move backwards.

The rope tightened and the yellow engine began to clank and pant and puff. His face grew very grim.

He began to tug on the rope — and slowly the tree trunk began to move.

The tree trunk began to roll and roll backwards, until it had rolled right off the track!

Tom stopped the little yellow engine and untied the rope. Everyone cheered.

Tom patted the little yellow engine who was looking very pleased with himself!

The passengers climbed on board again. Sam Squirrel scampered up another tree and changed the signal lights from red to green and four railway rabbits, wearing their Sunny Wood railway hats, turned up to watch the little yellow train continue his journey to Flower Valley.

'You can turn the fallen tree trunk into a woodland seat for everyone,' suggested Tom, as he climbed on board the yellow engine.

Tom sounded the whistle which went 'Tooweet!'

The four Sunny Wood railway rabbits on the tree trunk raised their hats and cheered as the little yellow train began to move slowly forward. Signalman Sam Squirrel merrily waved a green flag from his tree.

Tom looked at his pocket watch and whispered to the yellow engine, 'If we hurry along, we can still be in time for the Flower Valley concert.'

At last, the little yellow train steamed around the bend and into Flower Valley.

Although the Flower Valley orchestra was already in its place, everyone was anxiously waiting for the arrival of Willie Mouse, Maurice Mole, Herbert von Hare, and Prudence Pig. When they saw the little yellow train appear with their musical guests on board, they waved in delight and threw their hats in the air!

The Flower Valley orchestra, conducted by Herbert von Hare, played some lovely music.

The animals sat quietly under the trees and amongst the flowers. Willie Mouse blew his flute and Maurice Mole played his saxophone. Prudence Pig sang some songs and no-one seemed to mind her squeaky voice.

There, on a sloping hill in the distance, stood the little yellow engine who was smiling and listening to the music. Imagine everyone's surprise when he suddenly began to whistle in time to the music. Musical notes of steam began to come out of the engine and drift high into the blue sky.

It was getting dark when the little yellow train chugged back home towards Green Hill.

The lamp on the front of the engine was lit and some sparks could be seen coming out of his chimney.

High above them shone the first star of evening. It had been a lovely day . . .

They had dropped off Herbert von Hare and Willie Mouse at Sunny Wood station. Prudence Pig and Maurice Mole were staying with friends in Flower Valley.

Right ahead Tom could see the green signal light hanging from Oswald Owl's tree.

In ten more minutes the little yellow railway engine would be back home in the big cave at the foot of Green Hill.

Then Tom would climb up to his cottage, which stood right at the top of Green Hill, and have a mug of cocoa before going to bed.

The Secret Tunnel

Snow had been lying on Green Hill all through the winter months. So when Toot, the yellow engine, woke up one spring morning he almost shivered . . . The snow still lay everywhere, and it was deeper than ever!

All the flowers had gone and Green Hill was white and bare.

A Sunny Wood railway rabbit was already busy with a spade clearing some snow away.

Toot could see Oswald Owl brushing the fresh snow off the green signal lamp ahead.

When Tom, the engine driver, came down from his cottage he looked very grim. He wore his gloves, a warm red muffler and an overcoat. He carried his railway bag with a flask of tea inside.

The first thing Tom did, after saying 'Good morning!' to Toot, was to fix a red snow plough to the front of the engine.

'Toot,' said Tom, 'today we have to go on a long journey. Our friends, the animals, are so tired of the snow, that we have got to find a way of bringing back the flowers to Green Hill.'

As soon as Tom had lit the boiler, steam came puffing out of the yellow engine's funnel. After Tom had oiled the wheels he sounded the whistle and the little yellow train slowly puffed out of his icy cave in Green Hill.

With the help of the red snow plough, Toot the engine began to push aside the snow.

'We're going on a long journey,' repeated Tom. 'We're taking two trucks. Sam and Sid Squirrel are coming, and so is Rodney Rabbit.'

'I wonder where we are going?' Toot said to himself.

'In case you're wondering,' Tom went on, 'we're heading for the land beyond the secret tunnel. There is a story that Summerland lies beyond the secret tunnel. I thought we might be able to find some flowers there . . .'

Toot had heard of the secret tunnel only once before. He knew that to reach it you must first pass through a big forest.

Snowflakes began to fall again as the little yellow train entered the big forest. The tops of the trees were white with snow. Some of the birds living there wore hats and mufflers.

There were no signal lights or stations in the big forest so Tom drove the yellow engine slowly, always making sure that the track ahead was clear.

The fire heating the little engine's boiler kept Tom warm. As for Toot, well, he was beginning to enjoy his great adventure.

Suddenly Tom saw a snow-covered tunnel ahead. Icicles hung from the roof and a rabbit stood nearby.

'Hum,' said Tom. 'I don't remember seeing that tunnel before.' When he checked his railway map he saw that no tunnel was marked on the map.

'Well, Toot, this is very strange!' cried Tom. 'I think we had better slow down, don't you?'

Tom sounded the whistle twice as they approached the tunnel. Then he switched on the lamp at the front of the engine for it was the darkest tunnel he had ever seen. In the two trucks behind, Sam and Sid Squirrel and Rodney Rabbit had been playing I-Spy, but now they had to stop playing because they couldn't see a thing.

'I think this is the longest tunnel I've ever been in,' whispered Rodney Rabbit. 'It's longer than all the rabbit tunnels in Sunny Wood put together.'

'I wonder what can be at the other end?' said Sid Squirrel.

The tunnel seemed to go on and on and on. Only the lamp at the front of the little yellow engine cut through the gloom. It was a great relief to Tom when he saw a glimmer of light at the far end of the tunnel.

Slowly the light grew brighter and Tom began to think he could see lots of bright colours.

'Well blow me down!' he cried at last. 'I think I can see flowers! Flowers and sunshine!'

In his excitement Tom pressed the brake on the little yellow engine and they almost ground to a halt.

'Well, Toot, I reckon this must be Summerland,' said Tom. 'We've just passed through the secret tunnel — out of winter and into summer.'

In the two trucks behind Sam and Sid Squirrel and Rodney Rabbit had also seen the sunshine and the flowers.

'Where has all the snow gone?' gasped Sam Squirrel.

'It's magic!' laughed Sid Squirrel.

'I-Spy flowers and sunlight and rolling hills,' said Rodney Rabbit.

No wonder Toot the little yellow engine steamed happily into Summerland with a big smile on his face . . .

Toot had never seen so many flowers. All the fields and hills were bright with their colours, red ones, blue ones, yellow ones and white ones. Some of the grass was green and some was as gold as ripening corn.

The little yellow train had been bowling along as if in a dream when Tom, the driver, spied a castle ahead. It was the strangest shaped castle you ever saw. It had a funny red slate roof, white walls, a blue door and lots of steps. Then there were the flowers. There were hundreds of them, all different colours. Flowers grew all around the castle and it was easy to see that they were happy flowers.

As it was the only building in sight Tom stopped the train, and he and Rodney Rabbit began to climb the steps to the castle door.

By the time Tom had trudged up to the top of the steps he was quite out of breath.

'I feel so hot and stuffy in my heavy winter coat,' he muttered to himself.

'I feel hot too,' said Rodney Rabbit. 'But I like it. I wish we could take some of this Summerland sunshine and some of these lovely flowers back home with us.'

Just as he spoke the castle door opened and a round-faced friendly man appeared.

'Welcome friends!' beamed the man. 'Welcome to Summerland! My name is Mr Blossomflowers. What a day this is. I haven't seen a railway engine here in Summerland for more than twenty-five years. I thought everyone must have forgotten all about the secret tunnel. I'm so glad you've come.'

'Well, hum! Thankyou very much, and how do you do,' replied Tom, removing his glove and shaking Mr Blossomflowers by the hand.

'Mr Blossomflowers', he went on, 'we've travelled a long way through deep snow on the little yellow train, in search of flowers. My friends, the animals who live near Green Hill, are so tired of the snow that they long to see some bright flowers for a change.'

'Then follow me!' cried Mr Blossomflowers. 'I've got just the thing for you.'

Mr Blossomflowers took Tom to a golden hill, called Sunshine Hill, which was covered in flowers.

'Fill your two trucks with these special flowers,' beamed Mr Blossomflowers. 'These flowers are so full of sunlight that not only are they bright and colourful — they will even help to melt the snow for you.'

Sam and Sid Squirrel decided to stay in Summerland for a holiday. So only Tom and Rodney Rabbit were on board the little yellow train when, at last, it was time to go home.

They passed through the secret tunnel again, back into winter, and wound their way slowly through the big forest. But even before they reached Green Hill, Toot noticed that the snow was slowly beginning to melt.

The next day Tom and the railway rabbits planted out the special flowers in Sunny Wood and all over Green Hill.

In a day the snow had gone and the flowers were growing. Soon Green Hill looked as bright and sunny as any hill in Summerland — thanks to Mr Blossomflowers' special flowers!